Clint Faraday
book twenty eight
A Poisonous Personality

Gertrude Ainsley Midworth came from London, England, to David, Panamá, to get away from a bad situation. She is acid-tongued, critical, and downright malicious.

She knows no one here – and no one wants to know her.

So why was she being poisoned?

Contents

About the author

CD Moulton has traveled extensively over much of the world both in the music business, where he was a rock guitarist, songwriter and arranger and in an import/export business. He has been everything from a bar owner to auto salvage (junkyard) manager, longshoreman to high steel worker, orchid grower to landscaper, tropical fish farmer to commercial fisherman. He started writing books in 1983 and has published more than 350 books as of January 1, 2023. His most popular books to date are about research with orchids, though much of his science fiction and fantasy work has proven popular. He wrote the CD Grimes, PI series, and the Det. Nick Storie series, Clint Faraday series, and many other works.

He now resides in Gualaca, Chiriqui, Panamá, where he writes books, plays music with friends, does research with orchids and medicinal plants. He has lately become involved in fighting for the rights of the indigenous people, who are among his closest friends, and in fighting the extreme corruption in the courts and police in Panamá.

He offers the free e-book, *Fading Paradise*, that explains what he has been through because of the corruption.

CD is the discoverer of the Chadam Protocol for curing cancer.

Facebook page Ambrosia peruviana for cancer.

Clint Faraday, retired PI originally from Florida now residing in Bocas del Toro, Panamá, went into Peter's Bar in David and greeted the regulars he knew. Larry and Rick were on the balcony, talking with Aaron. Mark was at the bar with Dave, Clint's somewhat nutty musician/ botanist/ writer friend. George came in just behind him and went to the group on the balcony. Jessie was at the bar, and held up a cold Balboa. He nodded. There were four other people inside, and two natives sitting on the balcony. Clint ordered a plate of shrimp spaghetti from the kitchen. Dave was just going to Sasa for the second bar on his routine. Clint might run into him later.

Peter came in and greeted Clint, then went out onto the balcony to sit with the regular group there. Carlos came in and greeted everyone. Doug and his wife came in. Alan soon came in with Musician Jimmy. Jimmy said he was going to Sasa. Clint said Dave was there. German Jimmy came in and came to sit with Clint.

"Anyone new since my last stay here?" Clint asked.

"Not really. They come and go. Most of them are okay.

"I'm cooking up in Boquete now. It's a good market."

Jimmy made by far the best wiener schnitzel and several other Bavarian dishes Clint had ever tasted.

"Things don't change much here, I guess," Clint replied. "Whatever happened to Steve and Steve since I was here last?"

"They'll be in later, probably.

"There's one you will definitely want to avoid. She's from England, and is maybe the most, I guess you'd say vicious person I ever met."

"Vicious?"

"She finds things wrong with everything, and makes really mean and malicious remarks about people. You can't be nice to her. She won't let you. She's what we always called poisonous."

"We get them that way in Bocas, sometimes. They gripe about everything, then can't understand why no one will have anything to do with them."

"Yeah. You can be having a good night, and five minutes around her turns it sour."

They chatted about various other mundane things for awhile. Clint finished his delicious spaghetti and said he'd be back later. He went to

Sasa and had a beer with Dave and Musician Jimmy (So many Jimmies in the place that each was designated by some feature. Same with the Toms, etc.). He then went to the Parque Cantina and had a beer with his local friends, then went back to Peter's.

The mood was 180 from what it was earlier. A somewhat heavy woman was siting alone at the bar. Jessie walked by, and she snapped that her drink was almost empty. A halfway decent waitress would notice when a client wanted another drink and would offer it before the client died of thirst! Her voice was a bit grating and too loud.

Jessie ignored her. She was mixing drinks for four people on the balcony.

"You! I ordered a drink! Can I expect it tonight?" came from the woman.

"If you can't wait your turn, you can try to find a place where they'll put up with your silly crap," Clint said pleasantly. Jessie couldn't quite hide a grin.

"I beg your pardon?"

"Stop making an ass out of yourself and you'll find people will fall all over themselves to help you here."

"I never!"

"I can see *why*!"

"You! Barmaid! This man is bothering me!"

"It's the other way around," Steve, who never held back, said, coming in from the balcony.

"You Panamanians are the *rudest* people I've ever met!"

"Well, not quite, really. I'm not Panamanian," Steve answered innocently. "Panamanians will take your shit. I won't. You taught me a lot about rude last night, if you remember. You did that by example.

"Clint! Here investigating another murder, or just waiting for the inevitable one to happen?"

"Just visiting. How are things, otherwise?"

"I can't kick. Nobody'll listen."

"You are the police?" the woman asked Clint, ignoring Steve's existence.

"No. I just work with them."

"Well, you better do a better job! Someone tried to poison me, and the police won't even look for them!"

"Who should they look for?"

"The one who's trying to *kill* me!"

"Which is whom? I'm Clint Faraday."

"Gertrude Ainsley Midworth, from London. I have no idea who."

"So? What are the police supposed to do? Use their psychic ability? Can you even give them a wild possibility who to look for?"

"Who has that poison might be a place to start!"

"Which is what?"

"Which what is what?"

"The poison they're supposed to look for."

"I don't know anything about poisons. I haven't the least idea what it was."

"So the police are supposed to find someone from somewhere who's trying to kill you with a poison you can't name?"

"You're an ass!"

"That's a good one – coming from you!" Steve said.

"You're more of an ass!" she snarled.

"You'd know if anyone would. See you later, Clint." He walked out.

"Well! I never!"

"You already said that. How do you know you were being poisoned?"

"I was sick. I went to what passes for a hospital here, and the so-called doctor said it looked like a poison the Indians use to kill something or other, but he couldn't be sure. He didn't know much about it, except it was an alcolide or something they got out of a plant."

"Alcolide? You mean alkaloid?"

"Something like that. It looks like, if it was that easy to know what it was, he could find who has it!"

"There are hundreds of poisonous alkaloids from plants. If it's a common type, anyone could get it. Everyone knows about a number of them. Digitalin and those were known for centuries. Hemlock is another one."

"Even I know about those!"

"I see! If someone gets a dose of one of them the police should immediately arrest you as someone who might have done it?"

"You're an ass!"

"You said that, too. Have a good night!" he walked out onto the balcony. "I see that you've met Miss Congeniality!" Aaron said.

Clint gave him the bird.

<u>Second Attempt</u>

Clint went along the market row, buying a few new clothes. He always strolled along the street when he needed anything. As a general rule, he could buy the same brand on the row for half or less what it would cost in the shops only two blocks away. He bought some shirts and shorts and underwear, a couple pairs of chankletas (flip-flops) and socks. He needed a new black belt.

He took the items out to his car to lock them in the trunk, then went into Poderosa to get a lot of kitchen items and some towels, then drove to the Castilla parking lot and went across the street to the Office Center to get printer ink and paper and another 4G memory stick.

He saw Dave going into Romeros and hailed him. They were friends who met in lots of places. Dave asked about Tyna, Clint's wife, and the expected baby. He said everything was better than they deserved. They were going to stay in Cusapín as soon as the baby was born for a few months, then would go to Quebrada Tula for a few months, then to Bocas. They'd made arrangements for people to stay in the Bocas place when they weren't there. His brother's son and his wife would be there for two months.

"Your brother, the gambling addict?"

"Yeah. He ain't coming. He'd manage to lose everything he has in a week in even a little casino like they have here. He'd take out a loan on my boat and even my house that he'd pay back when he hits another big one. He's due."

"They're always due. They hit a ten grand pot and spend fifteen trying to double it. The only thing they double is the debt."

They chatted awhile, then Clint went back to the Riviera Hotel to check out, then drove back to Almirante, where he took the stuff he'd bought across the bay in his boat. He tied to his dock and went in to play and tease with Tyna. Judi Lum, his attractive nextdoor neighbor, came in and they fixed a great pizza-like thing Dave invented. He called it his Turkish Pizza. It was made with curried pork, and was delicious. They sometimes had his "Almost Stroganov," another invention that was basically beef Stroganov with a few added ingredients, Asparagus was the favorite, but was horribly expensive here. Clint made it with zucchini. They chatted awhile after the meal, then went into Bocas Town to walk around and trade gossip and such with people. They sat at the Golden Grill with a few regulars, then went back home. Judi met Ben and Earl, two other close neighbors, and went across to the Pickled Parrot in Ben's boat.

Clint caught up to date on his e-mail and other computer stuff, then he and Tyna watched a comic movie on TV starring Leslie Neilsen that was hilarious.

In the morning Clint and Tyna started getting things together they would take to Cusapín. They would travel, as always, light. They wouldn't go until next week, but everything would be right there to load onto the boat. From long experience, Clint knew that it was best to start early on that kind of thing so you didn't get halfway to where you were going and remember things you forgot.

At two twenty five Clint got a call. It was Dave, in David. "You remember that Gertrude pill? From London?"

"Yes?"

"She's back in the hospital. Critical. Poison. She asked the doctor to call you because you were already investigating the time before when someone tried to kill her."

"I am?"

"Doc Catán said to call you. I called you."

"Do you think it's something I'd give a damn about?"

"A lot of people are calling, asking about her. People in other places."

"So. Some obnoxious woman people will flock to avoid ends up in the hospital, poisoned, and a lot of people are suddenly interested. People in other places.

"Family?"

"Hmm. A couple claimed to be. To me, the telling thing is that she asked for you, a man she met for a few minutes in a bar."

"I have a free day or two. I'll come over there and talk to her. Maybe there's more than we imagine about her."

"It's your problem. Frankly, I'd end up telling whoever which poisons are most effective. The one they used is treatable. A lot of them aren't.

"I'm on my way to Punto Guabo. I can stay with friends there and finish my orchid classification reaearch to the Veraguas line. I'm talking with a small group of conservationists who will help with building a botanical garden second to none on the comarca. A lot of the Indigenos are inter-ested, but for the knowledge gained basis, not commercial. I'm with them in saying people can come to study, but there aren't going to be a lot of tourist trap businesses on the place. Most of the conservationists are in agreement with us, but some are in it strictly for the money angle –

which shows exactly how much conservationists they really are. Shithead greedy pigs!"

Dave tended to say what he thought. (Oh? You noticed?)

"It would have to be pretty big. The elevation for a lot of things isn't found close to the coast."

"The place we're concentrating on would be a thousand meters wide and six kilometers deep. We have elevations to about twelve hundred meters in it. I can put in a misting system that would let me grow the cloud forest things. Two hundred dollars for PVC. We'd use it at night. That's when the clouds sit on the mountains in the cloud forests. I'm not worried about any of that because the night temperatures are what we want with that extra cooling. It's a matter of four or five degrees for optimum."

"I wish you luck. I'm in."

"Judi already signed you into it."

"She would!"

They chatted for a couple more minutes about what was happening that affected the comarca, then rang off. He probably wouldn't hear from Dave for a month or more if he was going into that area. There wasn't a signal for celulars. Maybe he would use his direct satellite connection with the computer if it was important, or if he even thought of it. He tended to get lost in his studies.

Clint told Tyna he was going to head for David. A woman he talked to had been poisoned, which was definitely *not* totally unexpected. It suited her personality too well.

"That English woman you told me about? You care?"

"I'm curious. She asked the doctor to contact me."

"Well, I'm late enough that I can use the rest, and I tend to be bitchy, so it'll probably work out for the best, so long as it's for a day or two and not a week or two." They played and teased, then Clint got his boat and headed for Almirante and his car. He called, and had Lee save him a room at the Pensión Costa Rica. He was in David three hours and a few minutes later. He went directly to the Mae Lewis Hospital and spoke with the doctor. The poison appeared to be from a plant that grew in swamps near the Pacific coast. It was a milder form of hemlock. Midworth was going to be in discomfort for a few weeks. It had done some damage. Her diet was going to be bland to the point she would probably lose a lot of weight because she wouldn't want to eat it.

Clint went in to see her, but she was confused, and kept dropping off to sleep. She said she was better in the morning. It seemed they couldn't keep the place dark enough for the poison to be arrested in this excuse for a hospital.

"Let's get something straight right now or I go back to Bocas Town and you can go to hell," Clint replied to that. "This hospital has just saved your life. Not ten hospitals in the world have the necessary knowledge and machinery to stop that kind of specific poison, and none of those would diagnose it fast enough that you wouldn't end up a vegetable from the damage.

"You can say something positive about the place or you can keep your mouth shut. Got it?"

She stared blearily at him for a few seconds, then, "I got it. I know I'm a bitch. It's hard not to be. It's all I've ever been and all I know.

"I'll see you in the morning?"

"Okay. We can try to figure what's going on."

"I know what's going on. I'm being poisoned. I just want to know which of them are doing it."

"Them who?"

"Tomorrow. Family." She suddenly was snoring a bit loudly. The nurse came in and said she had sleep apnea, among a number of other things that would have killed a normal person years ago.

Clint went to the Costa Rica, then to Las Brasas for a delicious filet mignon, then to several places to talk with people. He was going back toward the pensión when "Marcheska," an Indio transvestite, hailed him and said he could walk him to the bar. Some redneck gringo tourists were giving him trouble.

He grinned and walked with him to the Texas Bar. There were a number of transvestites from Colombia performing there, and the place was packed with a loud crowd. Clint had a couple of beers, then went to the Costa Rica. He had to admit that the bar was fun. He wasn't even uncomfortable when several guys hit on him. It was what happened at that kind of place, the same as when he was at a brothel (only in the line of business. He never had patronized such places. He didn't need to before he was married, and now wouldn't as a simple matter of principle). The prostitutes would hit on the customers. It was, after all, how they made their living, and was legal here.

He thought of the different way he looked at such things in the states and grinned. Life was a lot freer and a lot less complicated here.

He went in and sacked out.

In the morning he went to the hospital early. Midworth was awake and in much better mood and condition to talk. She had been sedated last night and vaguely remembered him being there. She remembered her solemn promise to not be such a vindictive poisonous bitch.

"Maybe you'll see why I'm what I am. I'll try to explain.

"I'm down here to get away from someone in the family. I can see they have a way to know I'm here, so it didn't work so well.

"I'm very wealthy. I'm a widow who inherited more than twenty five million pounds. It is mine, exclusively, because my husband said the whole family were lazy leeches who didn't deserve the time of day from him, and that included his two sons and our daughter.

"I wouldn't be at all surprised to find that my own daughter was trying to kill me for the money and the land. She's totally self-centered, and doesn't emote on a normal scale.

"I always had servants, since I married Harry. I met and married him in Ceylon, and we lived for twenty four years in India.

"I tried to make friends of the people who worked for us, at first, but Harry had always been the British Imperialist type, and they didn't trust me. I understood why, and tried to overcome it, but they stole from me, and would do horrible things. It was to get back at the British, and they would not, under any circumstance, accept me.

"I would ask, at first, that they bring me my tea. They would pretend not to hear or understand. It would be boiled and sour. I overheard four of them talking in the kitchen about how much a fool they were making of me. They were talking about putting something very nasty in Harry's whiskey. I was just outside the entrance, and there were only those bead strings between us, but it was dark where I was, so they didn't see me.

"I decided right then that, as Harry often said, if they're going to stone you for stealing a camel, anyway, you might as well steal a camel. I started giving orders and demanding service the way they accused all British of. I found keeping them afraid they would lose their job if things weren't to my expectations resulted in excellent service. They actually respected me for having the spine to act like that.

"I acted like that for twenty three and a half years, then Harry was bitten by a cobra and died. I was suspicious of the way he died, but had no reason to think it may be that one of the servants put the snake in the back patio garden to get back at us for being Britishers.

"Harry and I treated everyone that way except the family, who Harry took care of. He always said they were a worthless lot and would die of starvation if he didn't do anything for them, and that they were family, like it or not.

"Toward the end he found some things that soured him against even the family. I think it's probably that he found that some of them were embezzling funds from the business, even though he was paying them ten times what they were worth and fifteen times what he could get the natives for. He was more and more bitter against them.

"When he died we held the funeral ceremonies in London, and he was buried there. We also had the reading of the will there. It was a shock to all of us! Everybody in the family got exactly one pound sterling and the hope they would now make something of themselves more than hanger-on leeches! I got everything!

"I told everyone they could hold their present jobs and agreements would be honored for things to proceed as they had been.

"It wasn't ten days before someone tried to run me down in a car on the street. It was a Bentley the whole family used. I couldn't see who was driving. I heard it close and jumped to the side. It didn't miss me more than inches!

"I immediately became defensive, of course. I had tried to stop being the imperialist bitch there, then someone in my own family tried to kill me! I went back to being the bitch, and have stayed that way.

"I was told that Panamá was a safe place, and that English was widely spoken. I could expect to be treated as a general tourist here, so I came.

"I determined not to be the bitch anymore. I was going to blend in and live a normal life among normal people. It was very hard to ask for things and not demand them, but I was progressing. I didn't try to always find things to complain about, as a matter of course.

"I lived for a month in Panamá City, in a condominium I rented. I didn't correspond with anyone back home. I arranged for a bank account here that would not report where I was every time I withdrew funds.

"Then I was pushed in front of one of those painted buses while shopping. It is sheer luck that they drive with the full expectation that someone will step in front of them and thus know how to avoid hitting a person. It was so close that it tore the sleeve of my blouse, but the bus just continued on. It was, after all, a daily occurrence to the driver.

"There is absolutely no one here who knows anything about me, and I had made no enemies in Panamá City. I decided perhaps it was a true accident, and someone had been pushing past and I was shoved onto the street. The sidewalk was very crowded with people waiting for the light to change. I vowed to be very careful and to watch, but to not react too strongly to what could have been a coincidence.

"A day later I was visiting the old section with my camera. I was taking pictures of one of those old walls. I was standing beside another wall I had just taken pictures of. I heard a scraping noise above me and jumped away as a large heavy block dropped to where I was standing.

"Those blocks have been there a hundred years. For one to fall at that place at that time was not believable for one second! This time I knew someone was trying to kill me! I couldn't fathom who or *why*!

"I went directly back to my condo and hid there. I had my dinner sent up, and was a bit rude to the serving girl who brought it, then apologized, saying I'd had a close call with death earlier and still had the shakes. I didn't know who would want to kill me, but someone definitely had tried to do just that! Twice in two days!

"She was most kind. She said things happened for a reason and blah, blah, blah. I'm afraid I was a bit short with her for that. These were things done, not things that just happened.

"I cooled off a bit and downloaded my pictures onto my laptop. I discovered that I had taken two picture of the wall I was stationed by and that there was a person in the background just beside the wall on the last one. He or she had her back to me and I couldn't identify her, but she was very fair-skinned and fair-haired. There was a carry-bag on her shoulder – I keep saying 'her' because of the hair. It could have been a man with long hair or a woman with shorter hair – with a British Airways logo on the side. It was very much like one I purchased in the airport. It is the only place they're available. The person with that carrybag had been to London.

"You can see the conclusion I immediately jumped to.

"When I went out the next morning, the gate-man in the lobby asked if John Smith had reached me. He had called, asking for me, when I was in the city two days before. He told the caller I would return later.

"The entire staff had been told there was to be no confirmation that anyone there had ever heard of me if there were any calls or questions. This person then immediately ignored the request and put me in danger. I was back in India and the servants were doing those things to aggravate me.

"I reverted back to that personality, and can't break out of it. I am terrified, and don't know what to do.

"They said you were a famous detective who

worked with the police here. I am in hope there is something you can do to make things safer for me. That you might find which of them are doing this and put an end to it. I want advice, and fast, and good."

"I think maybe I can do something. I'll try.

"First, no one at this hospital is to acknowledge that you're here. We'll make it seem you were transferred to another specialized facility.

"I'll check a few things and come back with a lawyer."

"Lawyer?"

"Oh, yeah!"

Clint went to reception and told them to tell anyone who asked that Midworth was no longer there. He found the doctor in conference with three others and explained what he was doing. They would make very damned certain that no one would tell anyone else that Midworth was there.

He then called a lawyer he knew and could trust not to stab his clients in the back, as far too many were known to do in Panamá.

He called the police station to talk with Tonio, an officer he'd worked with before. He asked that they get him a list of everyone from England who had come into the country in the past month, and who were still here. That search would be done by computer, and was fast. He would have a list of sixty two names and passport identification sent to his e-mail in ten minutes or so.

He met with Yony, his lawyer friend, and they headed to the hospital. Midworth was in therapy, but would be out in fifteen minutes, so they went to the coffee shop and sat to discuss what was going on. Yony started writing the things to be included.

When Midworth was back in her room, they went in. Clint introduced Yony, and explained: "You are going to make a new will that leaves everything except one pound sterling to who or whatever you like."

"I thought of that, but would it be legal from here?"

"It's your last will and testament, registered with the country," Yony explained. "This is more for some of the things that will eventuate."

"Things?"

"Your companies will be informed only that there is a new will, nothing more, so that anything they are holding now is outdated. The company bank accounts will be informed that they are to release nothing until the will is read at your demise, and will be supplied a copy."

"Ah! A copy that someone in my family will be able to read!"

"Thus removing the incentive to kill you, if that's what it's about," Clint added. He took his laptop from it's carrycase and plugged it into the wall socket. He brought up his e-mail account he used with the police. There was a list of names.

"See if anything rings a bell," Clint said, and handed the laptop to Midworth. She spent a couple of minutes reading over the names, then exclaimed, "Why both of them?!"

"Both of whom?"

"Sandy Evans and Gordon Fielding. Two of Harry's cousins who are employed by the export company."

"Cousins are a bit back in what we're looking for, aren't they?" Clint asked.

"Yes. They wouldn't be in the will, in any case."

"Nobody else?"

"Yes. Tabitha Midworth. She's our daughter. Harold Midworth the Fourth, one of Harry's two sons. Lawrence ... I haven't heard from him in fifteen years! I thought he was dead! He's got to be ninety years old now!"

"Lawrence who? I haven't read the list."

"Midworth. Harry's uncle. I thought he died fifteen years ago on that boat that sank just out of Norway. The ferry thing."

"Well, we have five suspects. I'll have to trace where they were at the critical times," Clint said. "Yony will draw up the will for you, we can have it legally witnessed, notarized, then registered. Explain anything you want included to Yony. I'll be back in about half an hour and we can make plans for when the heirs-that-aren't learn the facts of life." He stood and stretched, packed up his laptop, and headed for the police station.

He noticed two people standing outside of the

hospital he had seen before. He had cultivated the habit of noticing everything about a place. These were definitely not, if appearances can be believed, Panamanians or Latinas. The woman had a carrybag with a British Airways logo on the side.

He took out his cell phone and walked three feet from them, saying, "She's been transferred to the poison center in Santiago. Doctor Catán says they have the new process there and she'll be alright in two more days." He stopped to flag a taxi right beside them, though his car was on the side lot. "Yes. She was already transported, just two hours ago, so she should be there in about two more hours." He got in the taxi and they drove off. He told the driver to go around the back road and got off at the back entrance to the parking lot. He went to his car and drove out through the back ambulance entrance. He went to the police station where he spent half an hour tracing where the passports had been shown. Tabitha was on Isla Colón. Fielding was in Panamá City, at the Hotel Europa. Sandy Evans and Lawrence Midworth were in David, and Harold Midworth IV was in Frontera, having just arrived at the guardia to enter Costa Rica. He was on the computer less than twenty minutes ago when he applied for the exit card.

None of them were at all the necessary points at the times of the attempted murders.

Clint sat back and looked at Tonio. "What the hell is this crap? Murder by committee?"

Tonio laughed, and shook his head. "The reason for that should be easy enough. Everyone who thinks they're going to get rich when she dies is in on it."

"Then why were Sandy Evans and Lawrence Midworth ... I'll be damned! It's not him, it's his son, or something!"

"What have I missed?"

"Lawrence Midworth and Sandy Evans were out front of Mae Lewis. The Lawrence Midworth Gertrude and I were looking for would be about ninety years old. That one was maybe thirty. It's his son or grandson out there. Neither is in the will, or would expect to be."

"I see. Now you have to find out what's really going on. Something's a very long way out of kilter here!"

"A very very long way!"

Clint grimaced, and thought for a few minutes, then took out his celular and made a call.

"Manolo? Clint Faraday. How are things?"

"Clint! Que paso?"

"Manolo, do you have connection to find out something about a person from England who spent most of her later life in India?"

"Uh-huh. Easy."

"Name's Gertrude Ainsley Midworth. London. Her passport's number XXXXXXXXX."

"Just her?"

"And family."

"One to one and a half hours."

"Thanks. Hope to see you soon. I'm going to spend some time in Cusapín."

"Going to get smart and raise your Ngobe kids as Ngobes?"

"Something like that." They chatted a minute more and rang off.

"So? Who's Manolo?" Tonio asked.

"Interpol. When it suits him."

Tonio nodded. "So he'll get New Scotland Yard on it and get some answers. Fast!" Clint's turn to nod. He soon headed back to the hospital. Evans and Midworth were gone. He went in to witness the will that Clint would take to the notary with Yony. When they were outside the room he told Yony there was a problem because the notary was closed until tomorrow morning at nine thirty. Yony asked why. The notary was *not* closed!

"You know that. I know that. Doc knows that. The nurse knows that. Most of the town knows that. Midworth does *not* know that."

Yony nodded. "I didn't quite accept things

about her. What do you suppose is wrong?"

"I wish to holy hell I knew! There were very definitely attempts to kill her, and there's a weird combination of people here.

"Yony, nobody would dare to try to fake being poisoned with that kind of thing. It's too touchy, and the results can be for life if you survive.

"I can't put anything together about her. She's apparently got almost unlimited funds to have herself guarded, but she runs here to hide? Why, damnit!?"

"It really is weird. I'll call her and inform her about the closed notary. Do you think you'll have time to get enough answers by tomorrow?"

"I can hope!"

Clint got the call from Manolo. It was more than two hours. He reported that she had gone with her family to Ceylon twenty four years ago, the family went back to Merry Old, she stayed, met and married Harold Midworth, a local big deal in export/import. They moved the operation to India and stayed there until he died of snakebite that may or may not have been contrived. She had gone to London at his death and to the estate her father left her when he died at about the same time as Midworth. His death was ruled due to of massive coronary thrombosis and deteriorated heart muscle.

"Something else to consider now. That was a convenient death, wouldn't you say?" Clint asked.

"Which one?"

"Take your pick. Which one died first?"

"Ainsley. By three weeks."

"I'm working out a scenario. Is there any record of the last time she was at the father's estate?"

"Not since she was a child. She hadn't been back to England."

"Wait a minute! Twenty four years, both of them from England and they never went for a visit?"

"He did. Every two years, for one month. Her, never."

"Yet her father was there in England, where her husband was going anyway?"

"Father and mother, except the mother died of ovarian cancer two years before."

"I think I have an small idea. Thanks, Manolo. You've made a semi-simple case into one that's maybe twenty five years old, and complicated."

There was a pause. "Gertie's not going to be Gertie, is she?"

"I'm beginning to think ... not." They talked a little more. Clint asked if Manolo could get a certified copy of the original passport Gertrude used to leave England. It would be e-mailed within the hour.

He called Yony and said he could get something for him. "Tell her the fact she's not there at the notary means she has to put her fingerprint on the signature."

"She's not her?"

"It's beginning to look a lot like that, or something on the order. *Somebody*'s not who they're supposed to be!"

He rang off and went to the Costa Rica to clean up. He would have the camarones apanada at La Tipica tonight.

Clint printed out the passport copy Manolo sent. He would have that when he and Yony went to the hospital early to explain she had to leave her fingerprint on the signature. He fully expected it wasn't going to match.

"I talked with the night nurse," Midworth said suspiciously. "She told me the notary was open yesterday. What's going on?"

"It was open then, but I have to get proof this is your signature, and it would close before I could get here and back," Yony said. "I should have remembered that from when I made the papers to sell the old Vargas place. He was bedridden and couldn't go, so we did the same thing with the notary, then. We just had to get a fingerprint on top of the signature. That's all.

"If you'll put a print on this I can run it over and get it done, then we can contact the bank and company."

"How will you know it's my signature? That doesn't seem to prove anything."

"If there's a later question, they take another print and compare. If it's really your signature and your print, you or whoever else loses the contesting."

"Why would I contest my own fingerprint?"

"No. If you claimed the document was false and they compared, and it is your signature and your print, you lose. If someone else claims it's false, you win with the comparison.."

"Oh. That's reasonable. I'm just getting a bit paranoid because of what's happened, I guess."

"Quite natural. Here. Ink pad, roll it like this, roll it above the signature so that part of it's on the signature, and wipe the ink off your finger. If I'd thought of that yesterday it would have saved a day. My fault. Ten seconds cost a day because it wasn't thought of at the time.

"I'll take this to the notary and be back in an hour, if there's not a line."

He took the will form and went out. Clint was a witness on the form, so had to go with him to the notary. They stopped in the doctor's lounge and compared the signatures.

"Shit!" Clint exclaimed. "It's her!"

"Well, what now? I have to register this."

"We register it, I guess. Can you delay it being recorded for some reason?"

"Only if there's a contest from someone who would suffer loss for cause."

"Let's stop by the police station. I may have

someone who can contest for cause – if I believe their cause."

They went to the police station and to Tonio's office. Clint asked if it would be possible to contact anyone on the list fast. Very fast.

"If they're at the hotel where they showed their passports."

"Find out!" Yony cried. "Something is definitely *not* right about that woman!"

Tonio brought the list up on his computer and called the Iberia Hotel. Evans came to the phone.

"I'm Clint Faraday, and there's no time for any bullshit! What's with Gertrude? What's going on?"

"I don't know who in hell you are, and if you mean Gertrude Midworth, she's stolen millions from my friends with a scheme in India. We're trying to stop her!"

"By poisoning her?"

"That was someone who's not here anymore. We just tried to scare her enough to make her do something that will give her away."

"Hmm. You don't lose anything, directly. Can we get someone, a family member, here to contest a new will?"

There was a silence, then, "She can't make a legal will. They ruled that in London. Something about the way Harry had died in a foreign country from an unlikely cause or something. She might not be the legal heir. The will she produced Harry was supposed to have made was ruled in question because something or other wasn't done. She has to wait seven years."

"In England. She can make a new will here that would have to be honored anywhere. She didn't think you'd find her here. How did you?"

"First, get some family member here. Today. I can't delay this more than a few hours," Yony said sternly. Clint asked how they would be able to accomplish that. She gave him the cell phone number of Tabitha. Tonio called Panamá City and requested that they get Tabitha to David ASAP. Today.

"We'll want to talk with you. We may be able to put an end to this crap," Clint said. "Can you and Lawrence come to the police station?"

"Yes. As fast as a taxi can get us there. Larry's right here."

"You're at the Iberia?" Tonio asked. "If you don't mind, I can have a police car pick you up in three or four minutes, out front."

"We'll be there!" She hung up.

"Can you contact India? Some place called ... I don't know where," Clint asked Tonio. "I'll get Manolo to put us in contact with NSY."

Tonio nodded and picked up the phone. Clint

called Manolo and found that it was a little place called Tabukuni in India where Midworth had the business. He noted that in his correspondence with NSY. He gave Clint a name and word code and the private number to call NSY.

Clint called the NSY number while Tonio contacted Tabukuni, India. He asked to speak with Peter Kindleton.

"Speaking. This is a private number. Where did you get it?"

Clint explained about Manolo and said they needed some information fast about Midworth, who Manolo called about earlier.

"Harold Midworth. I remember. I have the reports ... here. What do you need?"

"Why won't Gertrude be allowed to make a will for seven years in England?"

"I see. Why does that concern Panamá?"

"She's here. She's trying to get a will registered. We have no information to deny it, but things just don't seem right about her."

"Yes. Here's what ... could I fax or something? We'd spend too much time on the telephone."

"Clint Faraday. P-I-P-A-N-F-L one thousand at faraday P-I dot com."

"Done. On its way. We tend to think she bumped him off for the money. We weren't able to find one person who would argue in her favor.

They all said that would be on the line of her lousy personality. The lady, excuse the expression, is not among the best liked people you will ever meet. I had an interview with her, or sat in on one, where she came across as the most venomous person I'd ever run across. I doubt she made one sentence that wasn't belittling or vicious about even her own daughter.

"I hope this will tag her ass, personally.

"Anything else?"

"I think you have her pegged. When she's trying to be nice it sounds mean. Thanks." They rang off. Clint went out to his car to get the laptop as the police car drove up with Lawrence and Evans in it. She started to say something, then grinned. "Thought she was something she isn't at the hospital? She's still there?"

"Don't try to kill her again. She's too mean to die that easily."

"That missile hit the mark!" Lawrence said. "I'm Lawrence Andrew Midworth, grandnephew of Harold. This is Sandy Evans, my promised. We're engaged."

"Clint Faraday. I'm here because she called for me when the latest attempt was made to rid the world of a bucket of poison."

"A whole tanker full of it. One of those giant things," Sandy said.

"Well, come on inside. I hope Tabitha's on the way. Gertrude's trying to make a will that cuts everyone out. I guess she wants the money to be buried with her."

"Hah-ah! If she can't take it with her, she's not going!" Larry said cynically.

They went inside and Clint introduced them. Tonio said Tabitha would be there in two hours. He'd had a tourist bumped on the flight that was loading right now, and the plane would be held the ten minutes it would take her to get there. She was staying at the hotel four blocks from Albrook and ran out as soon as she got the call. She had been prepared to leave at any moment she got the word.

"Well, we can all sit around and get some fill-in on the situation while we wait. A car will be waiting at the airport to bring her here," Tonio said. "We can do some basic work. I'll give Yony a police order to say the will will not be registered for twenty four hours for investigation. He can tell her it's the standard procedure with a person who hasn't been in the country for ninety days or something."

"She will think she's going to have the will tomorrow and can do whatever she was planning. She wouldn't be released from the hospital before that, in any case," Yony suggested. "I can say the police always check with the country of the person who wants this class of legal document. It was a simple matter of having the police there declare she isn't a known or wanted felon. If we need more time later, we can say England police say there is a question they will try to resolve about legal papers involved with the company. Midworth was, after all, a corporation.

"You know something? That might be true! If he filed the will with the corporation they have a say in final dispensation!"

"My god! All along we may have had a way ... I'll bet that's what she's trying to get around! The will read was never legal! He was a corporation, and the only thing not in the corporation's name was the private bank account of the wife and or children!" Lawrence cried. "She didn't think they would check on it, and could get a will that we would have to bargain against. We couldn't get more than half if we weren't mentioned in the private will. I think the original will said that she got the estate house in Shropshire and a hundred thousand pounds and the rest was to be divided among direct heirs! Grandpops once told me there was something like that, and that I would someday own a ten percent share of a million pound business! I was only about fifteen or sixteen!"

"She killed him for nothing, then. I just don't know why she chose the time," Sandy said.

"Her father died of a massive coronary. He knew something, and she had to wait," Tonio replied. "I think I want to see her birth records. Her father and mother took her to Ceylon and as much as abandoned her there?"

"She often said he was a vile person who had molested her when she was younger, and that it was her own idea to stay in Ceylon," Sandy said.

"Well, time to contact merry old England again," Clint said, and called Kindleton, who said it was an ungodly hour to get calls.

"I'm sorry, but there's still something wrong," Clint explained. "How can we get the birth records on Gertrude. And any other records. Anything about her father."

"She pulled that 'He molested me!' routine? She tried that at the session, but they shortly disproved it. She was trying, I think, to blame someone for her personality.

"I'll call the office and have them e-mail everything we have on her. They will never volunteer anything, so I'll make it an order that is complete. Everything and peripheries. Fair enough?"

"Thanks, Peter. Come to Panamá and I'll spring for a vacation in paradise."

"I've heard both that it's a paradise and that it's hell."

"It's what you make it. Ciao!"

They chatted about anything that came up and everything until Tabitha came rushing in. She said that Gordon, her fiancee, was on the next flight. At almost the same time Clint's e-mail tone came on. He'd left it on the server to be ready.

"Let me read some of this. It may answer a lot of questions.

"Here's the birth record. Born in the hospital in Landsing under Beverly ... difficult birth, and mother would not be able to bear more offspring in future ... attended grammar school in Landsing and middle school in Beverly. Normal student with personality conflicts. Contentive with other students, and had few friends."

"That wouldn't be noted if it was in a normal range. She was born a bitch and lived her life a bitch ... sorry Tabby," Lawrence said.

"I know how she is far better than you, believe me!" Tabitha replied.

"Let's see. I don't care what she did in school so much. She moved to London when she was eighteen to get away from her family, who she claimed didn't understand her or even try to. Married John Fordhampton on her nineteenth birthday and ... wait a minute ... she never divorced him.

"So! That's the part she doesn't want investigated. She was never legally married to Harold Midworth, and wasn't eligible to inherit a penny as his wife.

"Let me see. The will is here, somewhere." He went through hundreds of pages, then, "... total effects to my wife, with stipulation that our daughter and my sons will receive one pound sterling and my hopes that they will blah, blah, blah.

"She was never his wife. She isn't his widow. That's what she had to try to get around. Getting a will that made her legal heir ... she had that in the will. She wanted it to specifically state the money accrued and business was to be disbursed according to the wishes of her late husband, Harold Midworth.

"She didn't have any late husband, unless John Fordhampton has recently died.

"We can use this to get everything into the hands the original will stated. I'll need a clear copy of that, but it can wait for a less ungodly hour in London. Meanwhile, Yony and I can go to the hospital and have a little chat with Gertrude Midworth. I think we should also contact India and make an observation or two about the death of your father, Tabitha."

"I knew something was very wrong about all of this mess. Dad and I always got along, other than the normal teenage things a couple of years ago when I thought he was trying to put me in a cage and wouldn't let me have any friends, and he was a horrible beast, and I wished I'd never been born, and he was just hateful to not trust me after all he raised me, and knew I wasn't going to get in trouble or anything, and I wished I was dead!

"The truth, as I told him last year, was that I wanted to get laid and I wanted it to be Sahsa Forni, who was a god to me, at the time. Dad was right, in that he turned out to be another teenager on the make, and it didn't make any difference to him if it was me or any other stupid naive girl. I did sneak out and get laid, and he wouldn't hardly speak to me, after that.

"Okay. I know damned well she managed to have him killed. A cobra in the bed or something was always a method in that part of India, because nothing could be proven, one way or the other.

"Well! Maybe we can at least have her listed as a suspect in a death that is suspect! If that's true, what you said about the wife thing and the will, she can try to get enough money together to get home, because she doesn't get a farthing from

Dad's will. She's not and never was a relative or spouse, and isn't mentioned in the will!"

"So. Let's go have a little frank chat with dear miss personality," Clint suggested. "She has a lot of the money in a bank here under her own name."

"That's Mrs. personality. She was married to somebody named John Fordcar or something," Sandy said.

"We'll sequester the account," Yony said

"Good afternoon, Mrs. Fordhampton," Yony greeted. "You can see why the law here checks carefully on people who want to make certain legal papers. There will be no will for a person who is using a false name. Past foibles will often catch up to them in the process.

"Did you murder Harold Midworth because he discovered he was never legally your husband, or was it strictly for the money?

"Incidentally, you weren't mentioned in the legal will of the corporation, Harold Midworth, LTD. except to be listed as a concerned party. He left all things to his wife, which you weren't. That means, as he had no wife, but did have two sons and a daughter, that they will be thus declared the recipients of the will.

"So! Tell us why you waited with your little scheme until your father passed away."

"You miserable lousy goddamned stinking low snake!" she hissed.

"Now, now! I'm just a lawyer you hired to make a will and to investigate its legality. I did that, you must admit!"

"I didn't hire you to investigate anything, you slimy bastard!" she screeched.

"Please! Mrs. Fordhampton! Hold your voice down! There are *decent* people and children here!" Clint demanded. "The investigation's part of the process you hired Yony for. He did his job. We'd appreciate it if you paid his fees before your account's sequestered. After, you won't be able to touch a penny."

"Sequestered?!" she squeaked. "What the hell does that mean? That this corrupt excuse for a government gets my money?"

"No. Your child and his children get it," Yony said. "Clint, she's the type who would try to screw me out of the fees if she'd won this stupid thing. I'll just write it off. Maybe one of the legitimate heirs will pay. I did save their millions for them."

They waited for her to run out of curses and epithets, but it didn't seem she ever would. Clint shrugged and they walked out. As they were leaving, Clint said, "Oh, holy crap! She won't be able to pay the hospital bill, now!"

That brought on newer and rawer language.

"Let's get with Tabby and friends and see what we can work out to get her ass sent to India for prosecution for murder. The fact she lived there with Midworth after duping him into believing she was his wife won't be looked on too very favorably."

"I'm due in court in a couple of hours. I'll have to prepare. I'll have to miss that part. I'll get the sequester notice and deliver it to the bank."

They talked a few minutes more, then Yony went to the Ciudad Judicial and Clint went to the Iberia Hotel to talk with his almost-victims.

Lawrence was in the little park near the Iberia when Clint drove by, so he stopped and went to talk with him. He asked about how he became involved in the plot to kill Gertrude.

"There was never any plot to kill her. That was Harry Four acting out of desperation. I'm glad it didn't work. They won't send him back here for prosecution on a failed attempt. All they'll do is forbid him to return as an undesirable or something, I imagine."

"Not even that. There won't be any report. It would probably result in JH if they did."

"JH?"

"Justifiable homicide. It's probable that she killed her husband, and her actions against her daughter and his sons was robbing them of their rightful inheritance.

"Apparently, she doesn't know your father was a ten percent silent partner in the corporation, and you get that part, regardless. I think Harold

Midworth was an honorable person. How did he get tangled up with such as her?"

"The foibles of youth, I suppose. She set out to marry rich, and did. Harry was in Ceylon, and didn't have much social life. His wife of six years dies, a pretty young girl from England comes and shows him and his sons some attention, he falls. They have a daughter. They're in a country where they don't really fit.

"For the past ten or more years they lived in separate parts of that Taj Mahal he built. He had made a few friends, she didn't have any. She was always a nasty character who ran anyone away who tried to get close. She was convinced that everyone they met was angling to get their money and was scheming. It was what *she* was and she projected it to everyone else.

"Dad knew her father, and said he was damned scared of her. He was a baronet with a lot of land and not much else. It wasn't land that would produce more than a minimum. It wasn't even attractive enough to construct some kind of tourist trap. He never was able to make a go of anything there, and couldn't find a buyer. She looked on him as a failure. She wouldn't even write a letter. Dad said he was relieved by that.

"She didn't have a hard life. While he didn't have millions, he was comfortable. The rural quiet life suited him. It never suited her."

"So she kills her husband to get the money – well, he wasn't her husband. Why did she wait until her father died?"

"I suppose because he wouldn't have kept silent about her being married to a bum who spent ninety percent of his life in jail. I met John once, about fifteen years ago. He was out of jail and went to Ainsley for a few pounds to tide him over. I didn't know he was her husband or I would have made some noise. He's in jail now for armed robbery, fourth offense, thirty years.

"I think she thinks she can take the money and have an exciting life. She came here because of the laws and to meet someone, but she can't stop being the paranoid bitch. The minute anyone tries to be nice, she thinks they're after her money, so she starts the cycle again.

"I think she's quite mad, but not legally. This will drive her over the edge, you know."

"I suppose the bunch of you could be in some danger. Watch your backs. I'll arrange for her to be thrown out of the country. Maybe she'll be sent to India to face investigation in Midworth's death."

"Won't ever happen. They won't bother. It's too common there, and they don't like these rich foreigners. She'll be sent to England. She does still have her father's land, so she can sit there and fester away. She'll never stop scheming, and might convince herself that she'll get Harry's inheritance if she knocks off all of us.

"I met Tabby three years ago when she came with Harry to England on his yearly visit. We hit it off. We plan to marry. Maybe Sandy will marry Harry Four."

"What about Gordon Fielding? How does he fit, other than being a cousin or something?"

"He's always been close to all of us. He's the best buddy to everyone type. We like to have him along at parties and when we go anywhere. He has a lot of money. He doesn't mind financing trips and such. He likes us as much as we like him, and we do pay our own way, really. He will pay for one and we will pay for the next to where it balances out. He's smart in business. We start little things, make a go of them and sell them. Small things, but you can have two or three small things going and sell them off for a little profit and be very comfortable. Five thousand pounds for one of them isn't much, but five thousand pounds for each of three is a quite nice living."

Clint nodded. He said he wanted to talk with the others. He wanted to be sure they knew to keep a very close watch on Gertrude. Don't give her any opportunity to do anything.

"Yony will sequester the money in her account. She won't be able to get any of it. *Do not* pay her way anywhere except India. If you can keep her there, you're reasonably safe from her."

"You don't know her! She'll think of something nasty. She probably already has."

They went to the Iberia and spent two hours discussing things and corresponding with the corporation headquarters in India. It looked like things would work out well for a group of decent people. Clint was preparing to go back to Bocas Town and saying goodbye when Yony called.

"Clint? I just took the sequester order to the bank. Sr. Geraldo informs me she cleaned out the account not half an hour ago! She has thirty five thousand dollars, cash! She's not at the hospital. They don't know how she left without being seen!"

"Oh, shit!" Clint replied. "Thanks, Yony."

"What's up?" Tabby asked.

"Your mother has escaped the hospital and has cleaned out the bank account. She's a crafty one! Be careful!"

"Crafty? No. Cunning," Larry said meaningfully. Clint nodded. He went to his car and called Tyna to say he missed hell out of her and he would be another day or two. He went back to check back into the Costa Rica.

"Tonio, I'm worried about that bitch and those kids. They're damned good kids. She's dangerous, and she's probably over the edge now."

"We can probably find her easily enough. What can we hold her for? Leaving the hospital without your doctor's approval isn't exactly against the law. It's perhaps stupid, but not illegal."

"She didn't pay the bill?"

"She put up a deposit. She's still got three more days paid on that. She hasn't paid the doctor, but that's not a legal problem, it's his."

"There has to be something. You can hold her for ID check for a few hours, but ... questionable passport!"

"Say what?"

"Her passport is for a Mrs. Midworth, isn't it?"

"Yes. It's the ... I see! She was not legally Mrs. Midworth. She was legally Mrs. Fordhampton! It's England's problem, but it's still a passport using an alias that isn't clearly expressed on the document. Panamá does not recognize passports using aliases. She is in this country illegally, and will be deported at her own expense.

"It's a technicality. I usually hate them, but this one serves well, I think." He called in an order to locate and detain the person offering a foreign passport issued to a non-existent entity; (Mrs.) Gertrude Ainsley Midworth. She is to be detained under the file of (Mrs.) Gertrude Ainsley Fordhampton.

They could only wait. Clint called Tabby and spoke to her and Larry. They would be leaving for Panamá City on the one o'clock bus. They would take the bus instead of a flight, because they wanted to see something of the country. They would leave for London at eight o'clock PM the day after tomorrow. They were staying together in a tight group until they were back in England.

Clint went into town to walk around. He met Carlos in the park, and they talked about whatever came up, then he went to the Multi-Café for lunch. Prices were a bit high, so they were trying that again. They raised their prices too much once before, and lost so much business they had to lower them. Now they were trying again. Everyone else had raised prices about ten percent with the new tax and the price of chicken going up so much. It looked like Mult-Café was trying for raising prices about eighty percent.

Clint shook his head at the girl working at the cash register. She shrugged and rolled her eyes.

He went to the terminal to see Tabby, Larry, et al get on the bus. As the bus pulled out of the station he caught a quick glimpse of a woman going by in a taxi. It was Gertrude.

He thought for a few seconds. He had the taxi number, so called Tonio and said to have that taxi stopped if it went through the David checkpoint at Las Lomas. Call the bus company and instruct the driver to not stop for passengers before Tolé.

He went to the police station to wait. The taxi didn't go to Las Lomas checkpoint. He had an officer find the cab and ask about Gertrude. She had raised hell because she was charged two fifty for the trip. The driver tried to tell her she paid one twenty five to be taken to the terminal and one twenty five to come back to Centro. She hadn't asked him for a round trip cuenta or he would have told her it was two fifty. She had gotten out of the taxi downtown and had gotten another almost immediately instead of having him take her on.

Clint thought a moment, then told Tonio. He didn't know what she planned, but it might be a better idea to watch her. Maybe they could catch her doing something that would allow them to prosecute her and hold her here in Panamá. That would give the kids some breathing room.

He had another idea then, and said to check the airport. Maybe she intended to fly to Panamá City and do whatever there. Tonio said they had an officer at the airport. What should he do?

"See what she does next. If she takes a flight to Panamá City we can have her watched every second there. She is definitely going to do something illegal."

He waited. Four minutes later Tonio called to say she was getting her flight, but not to Panamá City – to Santiago. She had paid the taxi driver fifty dollars to forget he ever saw her – after bitching about two fifty for a ride all around town.

"Penny wise, pound foolish. The bus stops in Santiago for half an hour. She'll do something there. I can get there before the bus, but have it posted that I might be traveling over the speed limit. My car. Don't stop me."

Tonio agreed. Clint got in his car, stopped at the bombas to fill the gas tank and headed for the CPA. He had some traffic to Chiriqui, then was able to make some time. There was little traffic. The construction just before Tolé had traffic stopped and backed up for a bit, but a police car was waiting and took him through immediately.

He passed the bus about fifteen minutes before

Santiago. He would have some time, so pulled off the carretera to put on his Hanrady disguise. He would be waiting at the Pyramid when the bus stopped, but wouldn't look like Clint Faraday. He could see what Gertrude planned.

The bus passed. He was in his car on the way two minutes later, and passed the bus ten minutes out of Santiago. He parked a block from the station and walked to sit in the restaurant at a table just inside to have coffee and hojaldras. A police woman looked at him a moment, then made a call. Clint quickly called Tonio and said he was in disguise. Was the woman looking for him?

No. She was probably looking for Gertrude. She had gotten off the plane and gone to a hotel and inside and hadn't come back out. The officer became suspicious and knocked on her door. She wasn't there. She hadn't come out of the hotel, but she was no longer there. The police would definitely be looking at everyone around when the bus stopped.

Clint thought for a minute, then looked at the officer standing to one side. She was avoiding speaking to anyone. She was a bit too heavy to be a police officer here. They had to be in excellent physical condition.

She was darker-skinned and her hair was black.

Her eyes were light hazel, which didn't fit the complexion. The ears were too light.

Clint grinned to himself. He got up and went to the public restroom, just past where the officer was standing, stayed a minute, then came out to go to her to ask, "A que hora esta proxima bus por Panamá?"

"Si," Gertrude replied. "I speak English. Are you a tourist?"

"No. I'm police. Interpol. We're looking for an international art thief to come through, but I suppose you've been informed about that, and aren't supposed to let anyone know about it.

"Keep the eyes on the prize! We'll take that bus apart if we have to! We'll definitely tag this one. The whole crew is ten seconds away! Armand LeCoufle is on the way to the pen for twenty to life, only he doesn't know it yet!"

"We'll get his slimy ass this time!" she said.

"Yes. He's traveling under the name of Fielding, and we just found out about it when he was checked about something in India or somewhere. He's cunning, and damned smart. Nobody with him knows he's one of the most successful art thieves in the world! He actually got away with that Picasso thing. A hundred seventy million pounds – that's English money, you know.

"I don't know. I think I respect hell out of

anyone who could pull that one off. We can't tag his ass in any way for it, but this one, he goes. For a lousy hundred thousand dollar deal!

"Well, so long as we get them, that's all that counts.

"Get ready! That's the bus! Stay out of sight until this goes down!"

He dashed back to the restaurant and sat at his table as the big bus pulled into the lot. Gertrude slipped out to the road and hailed a cab. Everyone got out and stretched, then headed for the restrooms or restaurant. Clint went back to his car and headed for the little airport. About twenty minutes later, Gertrude came in a taxi and went in to book a flight to Panamá City. He called Tonio and explained what had happened. He said they weren't prepared for her in Santiago, but would be in the city.

"What did she say when you told her Gordon Fielding was an art thief who got away with stealing a hundred million pounds worth of art?

"I think she pissed in her panties."

Clint could beat the bus to Panamá City with time to spare. He chatted with some people he knew in Santiago, then headed for the road.

It might be very interesting ... he had an idea. She would get off the plane at Albrook to hear a news flash on the terminal TV.

He soon was on the road. The trip into the city was uneventful, if fast. He used the celular to make some plans with Tonio. Her flight didn't leave Santiago for an hour and a half, there would be a slight delay, and the flight would be in a holding pattern until a problem at Albrook could be cleared off the runway.

Clint was waiting in the terminal, behind a newspaper, for just one minute when the plane landed. He now had a bushy mustache and long hair and was wearing a loud sweater. He looked heavier.

She came into the Albrook terminal to wait for her luggage as the TV announcer said, "A late breaking story just in! A police and international investigator team has failed in spectacular fashion as an internationally famous art thief, identified as Armand LeCoufle, of France, but actually an Englishman was expected to arrive in Santiago on a bus carrying a famous stolen painting. The bus arrived. The thief got off. He was arrested. The bus was searched. The thief's companions stated they were with him from David to Santiago and before, and that they knew of no art or of anything else. They have known the suspected art thief for some years and, though they were in many of the places where art was stolen, they didn't believe he had anything to do with it.

"There was no art of any kind on the bus. Police know it was placed into the bus in David and know of no way it could have been removed. It is suspected that the bus was stopped twice, once at a construction and once at the province check point. The only times it could have been removed was in those two very short periods.

"Police are looking for a woman who was in some way formerly associated with the thief. She has disappeared. She is wanted for questioning in the matter. This station will supply identifying information as soon as it is made available.

"Repeat: the arrest of famous international art thief, Armand LeCoufle, an alias, failed in spectacular fashion only a few moments ago in Santiago.

"In other news, the rains are causing...."

When the announcer said, "Famous art thief, Armand LeCoufle, of France," Gertrude stared at the screen with a shocked look on her face. When she announced that the police were looking for an Englishwoman who was associated, and who had disappeared, she looked terrified. It was so strange that several people noticed her and commented among themselves. One close to Clint said the way she reacted meant she almost had to be the woman who had disappeared. After all, she was obviously a gringo!

She calmed down and went to get her luggage. She got a taxi out front. Clint saw a police officer nod to a woman standing nearby and a taxi immediately came to her. She got in and they drove away just behind Gertrude.

"Don't be obvious!" Clint mumbled. He called Tonio and brought him up to the moment, then got his car and headed toward the bus terminal. He was almost there when he got a call.

"I'm Solano, with the police. Tonio asked that I call you and keep you informed of the movements here of a Mrs. Gertrude Midworth. I am to take instructions from you, an investigation expert who is employed by the police here.

"The suspect arrived at Albrook. The planned announcement came on the television set in the terminal. The suspect hired a taxi to take her to Tocumen. They are now en route there.

"What is instructed?"

"She will now believe Fielding will be watched closer than anyone in history, so she doesn't have a chance to do anything about them.

"I'm thinking out loud.

"She will try to leave Panamá. I suspect she'll head for England for the ... where she can be expected far too easily.

"Watch her! She's planning something for when

they catch their flight to England, tomorrow at eight o'clock PM!"

"As you gringos say, ten four!"

Clint thought. She was nuts. What did she plan? It was something that would work on the bus and would work on the plane. That meant putting a lot of other people at risk.

Clint called Tonio and asked if he could find out what was missing from the hospital. Fast!

He checked into the hotel at Tocumen. All he could do was wait. If he didn't learn what she planned or catch her, would it be successful?

He found it hard to get any sleep. He called Tyna to chat awhile and catch up on the news from Bocas. Things were fine there. She and Judi had gone to Changuinola to buy baby clothes. Matilde said the baby would be born early, but healthy. Nine days. Matilde was never wrong. They had to be in Cusapín then.

"But ... should you take that trip now? Isn't it too dangerous?"

"Matilde says the baby will be healthy and will be born. She's never wrong." That settled that!

"Well, I'll finish here as soon as I can and be back. Tomorrow, I hope, but probably the day after tomorrow."

He finally managed to drop off. He woke up a bit tired, but was up to normal after his third cup of coffee. He went to the police station and met and talked with several officers he knew, and was introduced to more.

At four thirty the tail on Gertrude called in to say she had put a lot of things in a taxi and was apparently going into the city.

What now?

He waited forty minutes and was told she had gone to a travel agency and had booked a tour of Europe. The ship left Colón in four days. She was headed back toward Tocumen.

Clint went to the terminal. Gertrude came in carrying a small valise and went to the restroom. She came out, still carrying the valise, and went to the desk of British Airways to check the valise through. Clint spotted the woman following her and said to find out which flight that valise was supposed to be carried on. Find out what was in the valise. See that it was *not* on that plane!

Gertrude left. She went to the hotel to check out, then back to sit in the terminal for about twenty minutes. She went to the British Airways desk and requested the valise, saying she had to have something in it. She would let them have ten observers, or they could just check it through again.

She was taken to a small room, where she was given the valise with two people watching every move. She took a cellular telephone out and made a call to England, saying she would want the papers to her estate ready when she arrived, then replaced the cellular into the valise. Clint was watching on the monitor.

Gertrude thanked them, and left. She got in a taxi to be taken to the Europa Hotel, in the City.

Clint went back inside and asked the security officer to show him the tape of when Gertrude was in the room. He watched it three times, and was about to give it up when he spotted something.

"Run it to where she took the phone from the valise!"

She took out the small cellular, turned it on, and immediately punched the autodial, talked for about one minutes, then handed the phone back to the officer to put back in the valise.

"Stop it there!" Clint ordered. The shot stopped and he had them magnify it.

"So! Run it one more time, and I'll show you what she did!"

They ran it. Just before she handed the phone to the officer she reached into the loose pocket of the loose safari pants she was wearing, handed the phone to the officer, and reached to the pocket again.

"Okay, first stop. Magnify it." It was the phone

in her hand, showing plainly.

"Notice here." He pointed to a small red plastic tab that covered the recharge socket.

"Bring up the second." It was as she handed the officer the phone. He pointed to the tab. Gilda, the security officer, raised an eyebrow.

"Can you split the screen with both shots?"

She did that. The tabs showed clearly. The one at first had the red tab. The second had the red tab with a small black dot in the center.

"Dios mio! How did she do that?!" Gilda cried.

"She was waving her free hand around as she talked. She put her hand on her chest several times, then dropped it, then waved it again. She took the phone in her left hand when she turned it on and again when she turned it off. She had just waved and dropped her hand. She took the second phone from her pocket in her left hand. She then dropped her hand with the phone as she started to hand it back to you, dropped it into the pocket, and seemed to place the phone into her left hand to turn it off. That phone was already in her left hand, the real one was then in her pocket, she thanked you and left.

"Now, let's see what's in that second phone, shall we?"

"No. The bomb squad will see what's in that second phone." She called in a man who took the valise out. He found a good bit of modern plastic explosive that would detonate if the number was called. It was enough to cause the plane to fall into the ocean, where it could never be determined for certain that it was not a freak accident.

"Real winner, ain't she?" Clint said. "Pick her up and charge her ass with attempted heinous multiple murder and terrorism!

"I'm going back to Bocas and my wife!"

Clint looked at Tyna, and grinned. She held the baby, Clintonito Faraday Abrego, and glowed. He loved her so! That was in addition to the love he already had for her. He'd had intimate relations with a lot of women before he married Tyna. He didn't think he would be true to her more than the societal norm here, but was surprised at how other women no longer appealed to him in the same way. He would look at them and note that they were extra pretty or extra sexy, but he didn't want them. Nobody could compare to Tyna!

He talked a few minutes and went outside onto the porch on his little cabin here in his personal paradise. The breeze was cool off the Caribbean, and the sunrise had been spectacular. Basilio had gone to the mountain last night to get a reading of the sunset that would tell him the possible future of the baby who was born while he was on the mountain. He had returned to say that the baby's future was bright and gold with some pale pink and some green. He would be healthy and a good worker, like his father and mother, and would be popular and honest. People would tend to like him, automatically, as with his father and mother, but he would also be sought out when there was a problem in someone else's life. He would be ready to help people.

"Does that mean he'll definitely be successful?" Clint asked.

"No. How he uses the things nature will give him is his own choice. There is great potential for a famous and good man, but it can sometimes be inverted to where the person with the talents and abilities will choose a ... different path. It is to you and Tyna to steer him. That is and always has been the way of life."

Clint could accept that. It was along the lines of his own understanding and philosophy. There are no givens in life.

His celular rang, and he answered the international number in the caller ID.

"Clint? Tabby Midworth here. I just wanted to thank you for what you did for us. I was just contacted by a law firm who told me I have now inherited Grampa Ainsley's estate. It seems that a felon in prison can't inherit, and that it's intestate, so I own it. Taxes are high, but I have a lot of money.

"I'm going to marry a world famous international art thief, it seems. Luckily, he's managed to escape capture for many years and has hundreds of millions of pounds in offshore accounts in Panamá!

"We're planning to come to Panamá for our honeymoon. We liked it there. The only problem is that Mother's in jail there, but no one will hold her against us. Larry's planning to marry Sandy, so we might make it a foursome wedding. Harry Four doesn't care to go there.

"So! How are things with you?"

"Well, I became a father last night. Other than that, it's just another day in my personal paradise. Things are wonderful!"

"Father? Girlfriend? I know they don't make any distinction there."

"Wife. They don't, but I do."

"I didn't even know you were married. Congrats for both!"

They chatted. Clint spoke to all of them.

After lunch of chicken and rice Panameño, Clint walked along the beach awhile with friends. He was asked for advice about a lot of things the Indigenos didn't have in their culture (Thank whatever gods that may be!). He tried to steer them away from the greed for things the Latina and gringo cultures imposed. They already knew those things didn't bring any real satisfaction, but they were seductive, in their own way.

He got another call just at dark. It was Tonio.

"Clint? Just wanted to give you another short update. About the Fordhampton woman. You know she was sentenced to life here, and was to be deported to India.

"It would seem she knew a lot more about poisons than just having a poisonous personality. She made something with scouring powder and Clorox and gassed herself. In prison! It was stuff they have everywhere for cleaning, and no one thought too much about it. She requested that she be given something to do, so they put her on clean-up detail. She put the stuff on her cart and went into an isolation cell and never came back out. They checked, and she was dead. She left a note that didn't make much sense, a letter, actually, in her cell. She blamed her father and her husband for cheating her out of the millions that were rightfully hers and we all conspired against her here to lock her away so we could steal what little was left.

"Anyhow, she's no longer a problem to anyone. Thought you'd want to know."

Clint told him about Tabby's call, they chatted awhile, then Clint walked back down the beach to his little cabin. He held the baby a bit, and Tyna a lot.

Paradise is from inside. It's not so bad when you also are living in it outside!

C. D. Moulton's works are available on most major outlets as printed or e-books. CD writes the CD Grimes, PI mysteries, the Det. Lt. Nick Storie mysteries, the Clint Faraday mysteries, the Flight of the Maita science fiction series, books on orchid culture and many others of many types. Mystery, adventure, intrigue, science fiction, fantasy, paranormal, mild erotica, and factual.

www.ingramcontent.com/pod-product-compliance
Lightning Source LLC
Chambersburg PA
CBHW052223150726

48002CB00003B/1245